DC SUPER HEROES

DEMONS OF DEEP SPACE

WRITTEN BY
LAURIE S. SUTTON
ILLUSTRATED BY
LUCIANO VECCHIO

SUPERMAN CREATED BY
JERRY SIEGEL AND
JOE SHUSTER
BY SPECIAL ARRANGEMENT WITH
THE JERRY SIEGEL FAMILY

a Capstone company — publishers for children

RAINTREE IS AN IMPRINT OF CAPSTONE GLOBAL LIBRARY LIMITED, A COMPANY INCORPORATED IN ENGLAND AND WALES HAVING ITS REGISTERED OFFICE AT 264 BANBURY ROAD, OXFORD, OX2 7DY -REGISTERED COMPANY NUMBER: 6695582

WWW.RAINTREE.CO.UK
MYORDERS@RAINTREE.CO.UK

STAR38453

ART DIRECTOR: BOB LENTZ AND BRANN GARVEY
DESIGNER: HILARY WACHOLZ

ISBN 978 1 4747 3287 1
20 19 18 17 16
10 9 8 7 6 5 4 3 2 1

BRITISH LIBRARY CATALOGUING IN PUBLICATION DATA
A FULL CATALOGUE RECORD FOR THIS BOOK IS AVAILABLE FROM THE BRITISH LIBRARY.

PRINTED AND BOUND IN CHINA

CONTENTS

CHAPTER 1
TWO NEW GODS 6

CHAPTER 2
DARKEST DANGER 22

CHAPTER 3
BATTLEGROUND..37

CHAPTER 4
BALLS OF FIRE..50

CHAPTER 5
FINAL FATE.. 64

Years ago, in a distant galaxy, the planet Krypton exploded. Its only survivor was a baby called Kal-El who escaped in a rocket ship. After landing on Earth, he was adopted by the Kents, a kind couple who named him Clark. The boy soon discovered he had extraordinary abilities fuelled by the yellow sun of Earth. He chose to use these powers to help others, and so he became Superman - the guardian of his new home.

He is...
THE MAN OF STEEL
™

CHAPTER 1

TWO NEW GODS

"Mayday! Mayday!" the pilot called into the radio. "This is Metropolis Airlines, flight 319. We've lost an engine!"

The pilot looked out of the cockpit window and back at the wing. What he said on the radio was not an exaggeration. Something had struck the passenger jet and ripped the engine turbine off the wing. Stray wires and chunks of metal flapped in the wind where the turbine once was.

"We can't stay in the air," the co-pilot said. "We need help!"

"We need Superman!" the pilot said. "Where is he?"

The Man of Steel was nowhere near the falling aeroplane. He was far away at the bottom of the sea. A submarine was sinking and he had to save it.

Superman used his power of super-speed to swim faster than any fish in the sea. He was a kilometre under the water before he saw the experimental vessel. The pressure was tremendous this deep in the ocean. Superman could feel it pressing against his body. He was invulnerable, but that didn't mean he couldn't feel the pain of the immense water pressure. The submarine, however, was not invulnerable. It was in danger of being crushed by the strain on its hull.

CREEEEEAAAKKKK!

The steel plates started to give way and water gushed into the sub. It began to flood. Superman knew he had to get the vessel to the surface immediately. He swam under the sub and placed his hands under the bottom of the hull. Then he kicked his legs at super-speed, turning himself into a propeller. As his legs pumped through the water, the sub started to move up, up, up towards the surface.

Superman and the submarine broke the surface of the ocean with a huge **SPLAAAASSSSH!** Water sprayed into the air and drained out of the sub. After a few moments, the main hatch popped open and the captain climbed out.

"Thanks, Superman!" he said.

The Man of Steel could hear the cheers of the crew from inside the sub. He heard something else, too.

"Mayday! Mayday!" came a distant call.

Superman turned his gaze towards the blue sky above. He used his super-hearing to focus on the faint sound. Then he used his super-vision to spot the falling jet.

"That plane can't fly without engines," Superman said. "But I can."

The Man of Steel decided to put the sub down on a nearby beach. He waited for the sunbathing and swimming tourists to get out of the way before he set it down gently on the sand.

"Sorry, folks! I'll come back later and move this," Superman promised. "But right now someone else needs my help!"

Superman leaped into the sky. He used his super-speed to fly faster than a bullet. Soon he could see the damaged aeroplane. It was falling closer and closer to the ground. In a matter of moments, the plane would smash into the ground! Superman put on an extra burst of speed. ***WOOOOSH!***

He grabbed the front of one of the wings with his iron grip. Superman pulled back on the wing very carefully. The plane came out of its nosedive, straightening out bit by bit until it was once again flying straight. Then Superman flew under the plane. He put it on his back and carried the plane safely to Metropolis Airport. He was almost on the runway when he heard a loud ***BOOOOOM!***

At first Superman thought something on the plane had exploded.

Then he saw a fiery trail streaking overhead. *Strange,* thought Superman. *It looks like a meteor.*

Superman put the plane down on the runway of the airport. "I can't stay," he told the pilots. "There's another emergency that needs my immediate attention!"

Superman quickly flew in the direction of the line of fire that had been scratched across the sky.

"Wow, Superman sure is busy today," one of the pilots said.

"I think it's a pretty normal day for the Man of Steel," the co-pilot replied.

Superman chased the mysterious streak through the sky. It moved almost as fast as he did. The Man of Steel didn't know what it was.

Superman was worried that it might crash into a city and hurt people. Even if it crashed in an uninhabited area, it would cause a severe ecological disaster. He had to stop the unidentified object.

Suddenly the fireball changed direction. It went straight up into the air. Then it went sideways. This was not an ordinary object.

"Whatever that thing is, someone is controlling it," Superman said.

He used his super-vision to get a closer look. He was surprised at what he saw.

POWWWWWW! Something smashed into the Man of Steel. He was knocked through the air. He went twirling for a few moments before he was able to regain his balance.

Is this what happened to the aeroplane? Superman wondered.

Superman floated in mid-air and looked around for what had hit him. That was when he saw them. A hundred alien soldiers in anti-gravity armour rushing towards the Man of Steel.

ZAP! ZAP! ZAP!

They fired energy weapons at him. Bolts of destructive energy sizzled through the air like red lightning. Superman let the beams strike him square on the S-shield on his chest. The energy bolts bounced off his invulnerable body.

"Parademons from Apokolips," Superman said. They were the shock troops of Darkseid, the god-like dictator of a savage world. "You might be Darkseid's invasion force, but you won't get past me."

The alien soldiers did not speak. They were trained to fight – and nothing else. One of the drones pointed his weapon at a man hovering in mid-air behind him. The man stood on a flying platform that had an alien design. But Superman recognized the platform and the warrior who controlled it.

"Hello, Orion," Superman said. "Welcome back to Earth." The Man of Steel instantly recognized the second son of Darkseid. Unlike Kalibak – Darkseid's evil son – Orion walked the path of good. Having left home at an early age, Darkseid's dark influence had not been able to influence the heroic Orion.

Several Parademons were aiming their weapons at Orion now. "Need some help, old friend?" Superman asked.

"I am not the one in trouble!" Orion shouted. "I have come to warn –"

ZIRRRRRRRRRRRRT!

Several Parademon energy weapons blasted Orion at once. Orion fell onto the flying platform in a heap.

"Orion!" Superman shouted.

Faster than the eye could see, the Man of Steel used his heat vision like a laser to make the Parademons' weapons explode. The soldier drones scattered, powerless without their blasters. Superman landed next to his friend.

"Orion, are you hurt?" Superman asked.

Orion straightened up in his Astro Harness, the device which allowed him to travel across great distances – even space. He grinned at Superman.

"I am a warrior of the New Gods," Orion said. "It will take more than a few energy blasts to defeat me."

"Glad to hear it," Superman said.

Ping! Ping! Ping! The sound reverberated from inside Orion's harness.

Orion looked at a small device mounted on his harness. Superman recognized it as a Mother Box. It was a living computer built by Orion's people that gave its owner many amazing abilities such as teleportation. Even owners of the Mother Boxes didn't completely understand how they worked.

"Incoming!" Orion shouted suddenly.

BOOOOOOOM!

A sonic blast ripped through the air as an energy tunnel opened. Superman and Orion were thrown in opposite directions.

Then the sound and the tunnel disappeared. The sky was clear and blue and calm, but only for a second.

BOOOOOOOOM!

A woman as tall as Superman now floated in the sky. She had golden Aero-Discs attached to her boots that allowed her to float in the air. She wore the armour of a warrior and held a Mega-Rod that crackled with deadly energy.

"Big Barda!" Superman said. He recognized her in an instant. "Two New Gods in one day?"

"Superman! I have come to warn you!" Barda shouted.

Ping! Ping! Orion's Mother Box chirped.

Ping! Ping! The Mother Box on Barda's armour also sounded.

"A Boom Tube is forming!" Barda warned. She flew straight up into the sky. Superman and Orion followed her.

BOOOOOM! Another energy tunnel opened. A dozen female warriors flew out of it. They all wore Aero-Discs on their feet like Barda.

"Female Furies!" Superman said, recognizing the dreaded women warriors of Apokolips.

Just before the tube closed, out flew two more beings. One was a short woman with wild grey hair. The other was a muscular man with pointed ears and a permanent frown.

Superman knew the villains very well. But that didn't make their arrival any less surprising.

"Granny Goodness and Kalibak?!" Superman said. "Now I know what Orion and Barda were trying to warn me about!"

CHAPTER 2

DARKEST DANGER

The Man of Steel and his friends were surrounded by Female Furies and Parademon shock troops from Apokolips.

"It's an invasion!" Superman realized.

"It's worse than that, Kryptonian," Kalibak taunted. "But you'll be dead before the fate of this planet unfolds."

"Oh, Kalibak, don't give away the surprise," Granny Goodness teased.

"My half-brother Kalibak is right, Superman," Orion said. "I came to warn you that –"

KAZZZAAAT!

A barrage of energy beams struck Orion to silence him, but this time he was ready for the attack. He formed a force field around himself that protected him from harm. Orion was angry.

"Let me finish!" he yelled.

Orion launched himself at Kalibak and the Parademon troops. He used the weapons on his Astro Harness, speaking between attacks.

"Earth isn't –" **ZAP!**

"The only planet –" **ZRRRRRT!**

"In danger!" **ZAP!**

Orion stopped firing and turned towards Superman. "It's the whole universe that's at risk!" he said.

"Granny Goodness and Kalibak sent their troops to keep us from telling you," Barda added as she fired her Mega-Rod at the Female Furies.

"And now that Superman knows, what can he possibly do to stop us?" Granny mocked.

Superman grabbed the leg of a Parademon soldier and threw him into the other soldiers.

WHAMMMMMMMMMMMMMM!

They smashed into each other like falling dominoes and dropped from the sky. Then the Man of Steel flew at super-speed at the Female Furies, hitting one then bouncing to another like a pinball. They tumbled to the ground. Suddenly Granny Goodness and Kalibak had no troops to back them up.

"Now it's time for you two to disappear," Superman said.

"Impressive," Granny admitted. "You will make a fine addition to the forces of Apokolips."

"Don't count your victory before it's hatched," Superman said.

"Your defeat is certain," Kalibak said. "The Dark Lord is coming."

Ping! Ping! Ping! All the Mother Boxes sounded at once.

BADOOOOOOOOOM!

The air around them vibrated. A low humming shook their bodies and rattled their ears. For a moment, the air seemed to be splitting in half. . .

And then there was DARKSEID!

The ruler of Apokolips did not need a Boom Tube to teleport. He could travel through space and between dimensions at will. Darkseid was the supreme dictator of a hopeless world where all the inhabitants were his slaves.

"Ahh, I see that the Kryptonian defender of this ball of mud they call Earth has come to meet me," Darkseid said to the Man of Steel.

Darkseid floated in the air in front of Superman. His body looked like granite. His face was as hard as stone. His eyes were filled with molten fire.

"Meet you? No," Superman replied. "Beat you? Yes."

Superman unleashed his heat vision.

ZAPPPPPPPP!

Superman's eyes were as fiery as Darkseid's. Twin beams of energy hit the Dark Lord. *TSSSSZZZZ!* The air around Darkseid burst into flame. A huge fireball formed in the sky.

Darkseid moved out of the roaring furnace of Superman's heat vision. "These flames are nothing," he said, unharmed. "I command the Fire Pits of Apokolips!"

ZRRRRRRRRT!

The Dark Lord was hit with energy blasts from Orion and Big Barda.

ZAP! ZAP! Two Omega Beams shot from Darkseid's eyes. Their destructive power was legendary. They also had the ability to hit separate targets. The beams sped in two different directions. One hit Barda and the other hit Orion.

"Barda, you used to be my favourite Female Fury – until you rebelled!" Darkseid said. "And Orion, my son! You turned against me. You are another betrayer."

"Your evil acts turned me against you!" Orion shouted. The memories of his life on Apokolips filled Orion with anger. It released his warrior rage.

"Orion, no!" Superman warned. "He wants you to lose control of yourself!"

It was too late. Orion attacked Darkseid with all the power his Astro Harness possessed.

BADOOOOM! Darkseid was knocked out of the sky and towards the ground. Orion went after the Dark Lord. Barda followed.

SMAAAASH! Darkseid crash-landed in a forest and made a huge crater. Trees fell around him like toothpicks. The Dark Lord was not hurt. He did not have a scratch on him. He stood up but did not move to attack his opponents. Instead, he looked around at the scenery.

"What I seek is not here," Darkseid said.

Superman wondered what Darkseid was looking for. Whatever it was, it could not be good for planet Earth. In any case, he had to stop Darkseid from succeeding.

BLAAAAM!

Barda and Orion slammed into the Dark Lord. Huge chunks of soil and forest vegetation flew into the air. Darkseid shot his Omega Beams at the two warriors.

ZAPPPPPPPPPPPPP!

Superman used his super-speed to block the beams with his body. The beams zipped around him, bending to change paths, and struck Orion and Big Barda.

There was an explosion of fire. **FWOOOOOOOOOOOSH!** Suddenly the whole forest was ablaze. Superman used his super-breath to blow out the burning trees like birthday-cake candles.

The Man of Steel realized this battle was causing damage to everything except Darkseid. They had to fight the Dark Lord somewhere he couldn't hurt anyone, or cause more destruction. Superman punched Darkseid with all of his super-strength. **KAPOWWWWWWWWW!**

The Dark Lord went tumbling into the sky.

Soon, he was completely outside Earth's atmosphere. Granny Goodness and Kalibak flew after their master. The Furies and the Parademon soldiers followed their leaders.

"This isn't the end of the battle," Orion warned.

"Darkseid won't stop until he finds what he's looking for," Barda agreed.

"What is he looking for?" Superman asked. "He didn't seem interested in conquering the planet this time."

"This is what we came to warn you about," Orion said. "He seeks the Infinity Particle. Every planet in the universe will be under Darkseid's control if he finds it."

"The Infinity Particle?" Superman asked.

"It has the power to create an entire universe," Barda explained. "Darkseid wants to use it to reshape everything to fit his own dark vision."

"His goal is to rule an evil empire that spans all of reality, not just Apokolips," Orion said. "He wants the entire universe to be just like he is."

"Then it's a good thing he hasn't found this Infinity Particle yet," Superman said. "Do you have any idea where it is?"

"All we know is that it's somewhere in this solar system," Barda answered.

"Then we'd better not let it fall into Darkseid's hands," Superman said. "Let's go!"

"Superman, wait!" Big Barda said. "Take this."

Barda held out her hand. A small device was building itself in her palm. It looked like a little Mother Box.

"It will protect you from the vacuum of space," Barda said. She strapped it to his arm. "It's a part of my Mother Box. Think of it as a Mini Box."

Ping! The device let out a chirp.

"Thanks, Barda," Superman said. "I can hold my breath for a long time, but who knows how long I'll be beyond Earth's atmosphere!"

"The Mini Box doesn't have all the abilities that my Mother Box has," Barda warned. "But it will keep you alive in any hostile environment and will also let us communicate with each other across great distances."

"Enough words!" Orion blared. "My warrior's patience is growing thin! Darkseid threatens the universe. It's time to fight!"

Superman looked at Orion's eager eyes.

"We're right behind you," said the Man of Steel.

CHAPTER 3

BATTLEGROUND

WOOOOSH!

Orion fired all the boosters on his Astro Harness at once. He took off like a meteor. A fiery trail burned towards the heavens. Barda peeled after her comrade as fast as a rocket. Superman was right beside her.

They tore through the clouds of the lower atmosphere. Then even the tallest thunderheads were left behind them. They sped towards the black hostility of space – and Darkseid!

Thousands of Parademon troops in space armour were waiting for them in orbit. Kalibak had called for reinforcements. Orion howled with rage as soon as he saw them.

"You will face the fury of Orion and the New Gods!" Orion yelled. The Mother Box on his harness let his opponents hear his challenge. "Flee or die!"

The Parademons did not move.

"Foolish drones," Orion growled. Then he attacked.

SMASSSSSSSSSSSSH!

Orion slammed into the assembled troops like a runaway truck. The soldiers crashed and bounced against each other in confusion. It created a hole in their defensive line.

The hole opened in front of their leader, Kalibak. Orion zoomed towards his half-brother, firing the weapons on his Astro Harness. Kalibak fired back with a nerve beam from his Beta-Club.

KAPOW!!! The two energy streams met in a sizzling explosion of otherworldly power. It did not stop Orion.

"You always seek to prove your worth to our father," Orion said to Kalibak. "You will never gain his approval. In his eyes, he alone is worthy."

"You think you're better than I am," Kalibak snarled. "But I am Darkseid's firstborn. I am his second-in-command. You abandoned Apokolips. Traitor!"

Kalibak fired the Beta-Club at his half-brother in fury.

The strength of his anger increased the power of the weapon's nerve beam.

ZZZZZAPOWWW! It penetrated Orion's shields.

"Ah!" Orion shouted. He suddenly lost control of his flying platform and tumbled off into space.

Big Barda saw that her friend was in trouble, but she couldn't help him. She was too busy battling the Female Furies. Three of the warriors ganged up on her. They grabbed her arm and both of her legs, trapping her. Not far away, Granny Goodness laughed in triumph.

HAHAHAHAHA!

"Barda, you used to be the best of the Female Fury Battalion. Now they have defeated you," Granny gloated.

Barda struggled against the hold of her captors. She could not break their fierce grip. One of the Furies tried to snatch Barda's weapon from her free hand.

"I'll just take her Mega-Rod as a prize of war," Bernadeth said.

"No! I want it!" Lashina said.

"Who says either of you deserve it?" Mad Harriet demanded.

All three Furies started fighting each other for possession of the Mega-Rod. Suddenly Big Barda twisted out of their grasp.

"To the victor goes the spoils," Barda quoted. "Too bad you're all losers!"

As long as Barda held the Mega-Rod, she was in control of it. **ZOOOOOOOOOOOOOM!**

An explosion of energy from the weapon threw the Furies away from her. All of them were hurled towards the moon. Granny Goodness was left without her Female Furies.

"It looks like it's just you and me, Granny," Barda said as she tapped the Mega-Rod in the palm of her hand.

BLAAAAMMMM!

There was no warning before an energy burst exploded near by. A blur of blue and red shot past Big Barda. It was Superman. Darkseid had blasted him with his Omega Beams. The Man of Steel nearly re-entered Earth's atmosphere, but he pulled up just in time.

WHOOOOOOOOOOOSH!

He flew back to face the Dark Lord.

"You won't get what you want," Superman said to the arch villain. "Not this time – not ever."

"I do not understand why you protect the natives of this planet. You have the power to conquer them," Darkseid said to Superman. "They should be your slaves, not your equals."

"That's the difference between us, Darkseid," Superman replied. "To me, helping them is its own reward."

"Compassion is for weaklings," Darkseid scoffed. "You disappoint me, Kryptonian."

"I can live with that," Superman shrugged.

The Man of Steel hauled back his fist to deliver a super-punch. **THUDDDDD!**

Darkseid blocked the blow, looking bored by the attack.

"You have great power, yet your battle tactics are primitive," Darkseid observed.

"They've been enough to stop you in the past," Superman replied. "Are you afraid to fight me?"

Darkseid stared at the Man of Steel with a molten, glowing gaze. His expression was so cold and empty of emotion that it sent a shiver down Superman's spine. The Man of Steel knew he was looking at pure evil in humanoid form.

"Afraid?" Darkseid repeated as if the word was strange to him. "I don't feel fear. I create it."

The Dark Lord summoned one of his powers and suddenly grew.

In moments, he was gigantic in size, towering over Superman like a skyscraper. His glowing red eyes were as fiery as two volcanoes. His fearsome face rose up in front of the Man of Steel. Superman was no bigger than Darkseid's nose.

"Is that supposed to intimidate me?" Superman asked. "There's a saying on Earth – 'The bigger they are, the harder they fall'."

The Man of Steel flew at super-speed and hit Darkseid right between his eyes. **THUNKKKKK!** The Dark Lord was caught by surprise and knocked backwards. In the zero gravity of space, he kept moving. For a moment, Superman wondered why Darkseid didn't stop himself. He had the power to do it. Superman flew after his gigantic foe.

"At last!" Darkseid declared. He stopped tumbling and floated. "I sense the presence of the Infinity Particle!" **BLIPPPPP!** He disappeared.

Superman was super-fast, but even the Man of Steel was too slow to stop Darkseid. The Dark Lord had transported out of sight.

"It was a trick," Superman realized. "Darkseid was stalling the whole time just so he could track down the Infinity Particle."

"Where did he go?" Big Barda asked as she flew up next to Superman with Orion by her side. "Granny and Kalibak are out of action for now. This is our chance to combine forces and beat the Dark Lord."

The Man of Steel scanned with his super-vision but could find no trace of Darkseid.

Superman shook his head. "Darkseid teleported somewhere," he told his allies. "And he might have located the Infinity Particle."

"We must find him!" Orion said. "If we don't, the whole universe is doomed!"

CHAPTER 4

BALLS OF FIRE

Superman and his allies floated in space above planet Earth. Astronauts called it the "Big Blue Marble". Superman called it "home", and he was determined to protect it from the threat of Darkseid.

"The Infinity Particle is somewhere in this solar system," Superman said as he scanned with his super-vision. "I have to find Darkseid before he reaches it."

"There's too much territory for you to search alone, Superman," Barda said. "Let us help you."

"We are allies in this battle," Orion agreed.

"The more the merrier," Superman said.

"Mother Box will aid us," Barda said. "She can scan the subtle forces of the solar system."

"Yes, Mother Box can detect the movement of a single molecule," Orion said. "If Darkseid has left a trail, she will find it."

"Mother Box, locate Darkseid!" Barda said.

PING! PING! Barda's Mother Box replied instantly.

PING! PING! Orion's device agreed.

PING! Superman's Mini Box chimed in.

"Jupiter!" Barda translated. "Mother Box says that Darkseid went to the planet called Jupiter."

"Then we must go there, too," Orion said. "Mother Box, open a Boom Tube!"

The space in front of them rippled, and then opened up. **WOOOOOSH!**

The three heroes felt the force of the tunnel opening up. Barda flew into the tunnel. Orion was right behind her. Superman was about to follow them when an energy blast hit him in the back. ***ZAPPPPP!***

He turned around and saw that the armies of Kalibak and Granny Goodness were rushing towards him. "We've got company," Superman warned his friends in the Boom Tube.

"There is no honour in shooting an opponent in the back," Orion declared. He flew his platform between Superman and the Parademon troops. "Cowards! Witness my wrath!"

ZAP! ZAP! Orion fired the weapons on his Astro Harness. A halo of raw energy surrounded him. Multiple beams shot out at the advancing enemy. Superman added his heat vision to the assault. The line of Parademon soldiers faltered and fell.

"Never leave mindless male drones to do a job Female Furies can do better," Granny Goodness boasted. She pointed at Superman and Orion. "Furies, bring those boys to Granny. I want to teach them a lesson."

The female warriors of Apokolips rushed towards the two heroes.

Mad Harriet laughed with wicked glee. Lashina swung her energy whip in electrified circles. The expressions on their faces made Superman think they were really going to enjoy this fight. The Man of Steel looked over at Orion and saw the same kind of wild smile on his lips.

"Orion! We can't waste time fighting here," Superman said. "Darkseid is our priority target."

"Battle is in my blood!" Orion declared hotly. "I must fight!"

"Not right now," Superman said between firing laser-sharp blasts of his heat vision.

POP! TSSSZZZZZ! The Mother Boxes that Kalibak and Granny Goodness wore on their armour now had holes burned into them, thanks to Superman's aim.

The miraculous devices were disabled. Their life-support systems started to fail.

"That will keep them too busy to follow us," Superman told Orion. "Let's get to Jupiter!"

The Man of Steel did not let his friend argue. He dragged Orion into the Boom Tube. There was no sense of time or distance inside the inter-dimensional tunnel. The heroes were in one place, and then they were in another place. The first thing they saw on the other side was Big Barda.

"What kept you?" she asked. "I thought you were right behind me."

"Parademons and Female Furies," Superman answered. "Where's Darkseid?"

"There," Barda pointed.

The Dark Lord of Apokolips hovered in orbit above the swirling gases of Jupiter. He did not move. He did not react to the appearance of the heroes.

"He knows we're here," Barda said. "He does not seem to care."

"I'm going to make him care in just a minute," Superman said.

The Man of Steel flew towards the Dark Lord. Orion powered up his Astro Harness and followed. Big Barda raised her Mega-Rod and joined her comrades. The trio ploughed into Darkseid at full speed.

KLANG!

It felt like they'd hit a moon made of iron. They bounced off the Dark Lord, each going in a different direction. The impact disturbed Darkseid's concentration.

Darkseid blinked his volcanic eyes and looked around. That's when he saw Superman.

"Ah, Kryptonian. Are you here to challenge me for possession of the Infinity Particle?" he asked. "Perhaps you want to rule this universe after all."

"No, I don't want the Infinity Particle," Superman said. "I just don't want *you* to have it."

"Then it is a challenge, after all," the Dark Lord decided. "Whoever gets the Infinity Particle first, wins!"

Darkseid's molten eyes blazed. The twin volcanoes became suns.

ZAP ZAP! Two fiery Omega Beams shot towards the upper layers of Jupiter's gaseous atmosphere.

They hit the Great Red Spot. The famous feature was three times the size of Earth. Now it was on fire. The spinning vortex caught the flames. The fire started to spread.

FWOOOOSSSSSSSSSSH! Suddenly the atmosphere of Jupiter ignited! The entire surface of the gas planet looked like the sun. Curling tendrils of super-hot plasma reached out into space.

"You have a choice, Superman," Darkseid said. "You can save this planet from destruction, or you can try to stop me from reaching the Infinity Particle. It's your decision."

The Dark Lord plunged into the burning atmosphere. Superman knew if he didn't put out this molecular fire, then Jupiter's mass would burn away, destroying the gravitational balance of the solar system.

But if the Dark Lord got hold of the Infinity Particle, the entire universe was doomed.

"Superman! What are you waiting for?" Orion said. He had returned with Big Barda.

"Go after Darkseid," Barda said. "We'll take care of the molecular fire."

Superman dived into the blazing atmosphere of Jupiter. Barda and Orion watched him disappear, then turned to look at each other.

"Do you know how we're going to put out this fire?" Orion asked his companion.

"We'll think of something," Barda replied. "But I had to convince Superman to go after Darkseid. He's the only one of us who can defeat him."

The Man of Steel descended through the thick bands of hydrogen gas that made up the top layers of the planet's atmosphere. He was glad to see that the fire did not go below that level. The flames just skimmed the top. It was like a fire burning on an oil slick – for now.

Superman followed Darkseid down through the brown bands of sulphur and ammonia clouds. It was easy to see where the Dark Lord had gone. He had left a swirling trail through the churning clouds.

Superman flew out of the thick brown clouds and into a clear zone. He flew right into a violent windstorm. He was caught by surprise and tumbled like a leaf. He had no control at all! Jupiter was a super-size planet and had super-size storms. The Man of Steel was carried along with the current of high-velocity wind.

Bolts of lightning sizzled between the band of clouds above Superman and the layers below him.

KRACKABOOOOM!

A claw of electrified atmosphere almost hit the Man of Steel. Usually lightning did not worry him, but the strength of these planetary bolts might damage the Mini Box. If it got damaged, he would be in serious trouble.

Superman knew he had to escape the storm!

CHAPTER 5

FINAL FATE

If this were a hurricane it would be a Category 200! Superman thought as he battled Jupiter's fierce winds.

Finally, he gained control and headed downwards. Below him was another layer of clouds. But when Superman entered them he discovered they weren't clouds at all. He was in a layer of slush. The extreme pressure of the atmosphere at this depth was turning the gases into liquid.

The sunlight disappeared the moment Superman entered the slush layer.

Even though he was on the daylight side of Jupiter, the sun was more than 700 million kilometres away. It was a faint speck in space. Its light could not penetrate the slush layer.

Superman flew through thick skies that were as black as night. The Man of Steel had to work as fast as possible. His powers would start dwindling the longer he was away from the golden rays of the sun.

"I better turn on the headlights," Superman joked to himself as he switched to X-ray vision.

The Man of Steel flew down through the dark, slushy fog of Jupiter's dense atmosphere. The pressure got stronger and stronger. It was the same thing that happened in the oceans on Earth.

Superman kept scanning for any sign of Darkseid. He had lost track of the Dark Lord when he was blown off course by the windstorm.

All Superman could see with his X-ray vision was hydrogen rain.

"I know he's down there somewhere," Superman said to himself. "He must still be looking for the Infinity Particle. That means I still have a chance to stop him."

Suddenly Superman spotted a solid mass heading for the planet's core.

"There you are," Superman said as he increased his speed towards the object.

POWWWW!

Superman smashed into Darkseid. The Dark Lord went spinning sideways.

BAAAAM!

Superman hit Darkseid with both of his fists. The villain was thrown high into the atmosphere. The Dark Lord was still as big as a mountain, but Superman punched him with all of his super-strength.

He was heading for the core, the Man of Steel realized. *The Infinity Particle must be there. I have to keep him away from it.*

The Man of Steel pounded his opponent with hammering blows. The Dark Lord did nothing to defend himself.

"Your efforts to keep me from the Infinity Particle are useless," Darkseid sneered. "It is within my grasp."

"You don't have it yet," Superman said. "And I'm not going to let you get it."

Superman flew straight into Darkseid's gigantic body. It was like hitting an asteroid. Superman hit him again and again. Each time Superman landed a blow, Darkseid was thrown higher into the atmosphere.

The Dark Lord did not care about Superman's attack. His focus was on possessing the Infinity Particle, until he realized that Superman was driving him further and further away from it.

ZAPPPP! ZAPPPP! Darkseid fired his Omega Beams at Superman. A force field formed in front of the Man of Steel and deflected the beams. Both Superman and Darkseid were surprised.

Ping! The Mini Box on Superman's wrist sounded.

"You have the protection of a Mother Box," Darkseid said. "I am impressed. They do not give their aid to just anyone."

Superman was glad Darkseid didn't know that it was only a Mini Box and did not have the full powers of the Mother Box.

"But it does not matter," Darkseid decided. "You cannot stand in my way. The Infinity Particle – and the universe – will be mine."

Darkseid fired the Omega Beams again, but not at Superman. He fired them towards the planet's core. It was like dropping a lit match into petrol. **FWOOOOOOSH!** Superman and Darkseid were engulfed by a molecular fire.

Superman flew out of the flames. Darkseid did not move. He laughed at Superman.

"Kryptonian coward!" Darkseid growled. "Your retreat secures my victory."

The Dark Lord sank into the dense liquid core of Jupiter. That's when he saw a brilliant speck of light flare up. Soon, it was as bright as a supernova.

Darkseid knew it was the Infinity Particle. His evil heart actually beat faster with excitement.

Darkseid reached out to take the Infinity Particle in his dark hand. Suddenly he stopped. His fiery red eyes widened in amazement when he saw the Man of Steel holding the Infinity Particle between his hands. Its light was brilliant between his fingers.

"You said whoever reaches the Infinity Particle first, wins, right?" Superman said.

Darkseid was not about to admit defeat. "I will crush you like an Apokolips slime bug and take the Infinity Particle from your fingers," Darkseid threatened.

He reached out with one monstrous hand and grabbed Superman.

The moment Darkseid touched the Man of Steel, the universe went blank. There was no Jupiter. There was no space vacuum. There was only Superman and Darkseid locked in possession of the Infinity Particle.

"I have the power to shape the universe!" Darkseid declared. "I command the Infinity Particle!"

Suddenly Superman and the Dark Lord were standing on Earth. It was not a planet that Superman recognized. The ground was scorched by fire.

There were giant flame pits filled with people. They cried out in fear when they saw Darkseid.

"This is more like it," Darkseid said.

"Is this how you think the universe should be?" Superman asked. "I have a different vision."

Suddenly they were standing on a planet that looked like a garden. There were trees and plants full of flowers. The sky was bright blue and sunny. The people were happy and laughing.

"No!" Darkseid protested. He changed the universe back into a chaotic, fiery world.

"Yes," Superman insisted. He made the universe bright again.

The two opponents went back and forth.

Entire universes were created and destroyed, then created again – all within seconds. Reality pulsed like a heartbeat. Dark. Light. Horror. Happiness.

"Enough," Superman said. Suddenly everything went blank again. "There can be only one universe."

"On that point, we agree," Darkseid said. "So surrender the Infinity Particle to me!"

Superman looked sadly at the brilliant speck of light in his hands. He appreciated the beauty and the power that was about to be lost forever.

CRUNCH! Superman crushed the Infinity Particle between his super-strong hands.

The light dimmed, then died.

NOOOOOOOOOOOOOOOOOOO!

Darkseid shouted in anger.

The atoms of the destroyed Infinity Particle were swept up into the molecular fire that burned over their heads.

SWOOOOOOOOOOOOOSH!

The flames consumed the Infinity Particle completely. It disappeared forever.

"You fool!" Darkseid said. "You've ruined everything!"

Before Superman could respond, Darkseid teleported back to Apokolips. The Man of Steel was left floating all by himself in the burning heart of Jupiter. "I guess it's up to me to clean up the mess Darkseid made," he said with a sigh.

WOOOOOOOOOOOOOOSH!

Superman started to spin at super-speed. His rapid spinning began to create a red and blue tornado. Slowly but surely, it sucked up the molecular fire into a massive vortex.

Shifting his hands, the Man of Steel was able to guide the vortex to the surface of the planet. Carefully, Superman used it like a vacuum cleaner to siphon off the fire that was burning brightly across the surface.

CRACKLE! CRACKLE!

Then he let the blazing molecules disperse harmlessly into the vast emptiness of space. The fire had been put out.

"Superman!" Big Barda said as she flew to his side. "You defeated Darkseid! His allies have fled."

"The Dark Lord will rise again," Orion added as he joined his companions. "But for now, we may rest."

"Yes, the universe is safe for now," Superman assured them. "Thank you for your help."

"We will always be your allies," Barda promised.

The three friends said goodbye. Barda and Orion opened a Boom Tube and returned to their home. Superman floated in orbit around Jupiter. He looked at the distant sun. It was a long way back to planet Earth.

Ping! Ping! Ping! The Mini Box sounded. Suddenly a Boom Tube opened in front of Superman.

"Thanks, Mini Box," he said. "This will get me home even faster."

Superman quickly stepped into the tunnel. He flew through space and time.

KIRRRSSSSH!

The next thing he knew, Superman was stepping out of it on Earth. The tube closed with a ***BOOOOM!***

Before he could even take a breath of fresh air, Superman heard something. "Help! Help!" came a distant, desperate cry.

The Man of Steel scanned for the location of the sound with his super-vision. He saw a bus full of schoolchildren teetering over the edge of a damaged bridge.

"Nice to have things back to normal," Superman said with a grin.

ZOOOOOOOM!

He flew to the rescue.

DARKSEID

Real Name:
Uxas

Occupation:
Dictator

Base:
Apokolips

Height:
2.6 metres

Weight:
820 kilograms

Eyes:
Red

Hair:
None

Uxas was the son of the King and Queen of Apokolips, and was second in line to the throne. When he came of age, he killed his older brother, Drax, claiming the throne for himself – as well as the fabled Omega Force. The incredible object transformed Uxas into a rock-like creature, making him nearly impervious to harm. Now, as Darkseid, he rules Apokolips with an iron fist, and aims to take down the Man of Steel, his only true threat.

- Darkseid is nearly invulnerable. However, incredible physical force, such as a punch from the Man of Steel himself, can weaken or even injure Darkseid.
- As one of the New Gods, Darkseid's body is not subject to disease or aging. He is considered by most to be immortal.
- Injuring Darkseid is difficult enough, but even when he is actually hurt, he's capable of regenerating his body at an incredible pace.
- Darkseid uses his super-strength and endurance to wear down his opponents in battle. He can also shoot Omega Beams, or laser-like blasts, from his eyes (this ability is quite similar to Superman's heat vision).

BIOGRAPHIES

LAURIE S. SUTTON has read comics since she was a child. She grew up to become an editor for Marvel, DC Comics, Starblaze and Tekno Comics. She has written *Adam Strange* for DC, *Star Trek: Voyager* for Marvel, plus *Star Trek: Deep Space Nine* and *Witch Hunter* for Malibu Comics. There are long boxes of comics in her wardrobe where there should be clothing and shoes. Laurie has lived all over the world, and currently resides in Florida, USA.

LUCIANO VECCHIO was born in 1982 and currently lives in Buenos Aires, Argentina. With experience in illustration, animation and comics, his works have been published in the UK, Spain, USA, France and Argentina. Credits include *Ben 10* (DC Comics), *Cruel Thing* (Norma), *Unseen Tribe* (Zuda Comics) and *Sentinels* (Drumfish Productions).

GLOSSARY

atmosphere mixture of gases that surround a planet

betrayer someone who is disloyal or lets a person down

descended climbed down or went down to a lower level

drones robots that function as servants or soldiers

exaggeration making something seem bigger or more important than it is

experimental something that is being tested to see how it works

invulnerable unable to be harmed or damaged

legendary amazing, or something from a legend

rage violent anger

unleashed released something that had been controlled

DISCUSSION QUESTIONS

1. There are many characters in this book. Which one is your favourite? Give reasons for your answer.
2. If you could travel through space like the heroes and villains in this book, which planet would you want to visit? Why?
3. This book has ten illustrations. Which one is your favourite? Why?

WRITING PROMPTS

1. Superman displays many superpowers in this book, including heat vision, super-strength and invulnerability. Create a new superpower for Superman. What's it called? What does it do? Write about it, then draw a picture of it in action.

2. Almost everyone has flaws. Orion, for example, gets angry too easily. What are your flaws? What are some good ways to limit your flaws?

3. If you had an Infinity Particle, what kind of universe would you create? Write about your universe.

LOOK FOR MORE